When Mum T MONSTER A

Joanna Harrison

Collins

An Imprint of HarperCollins*Publishers*

For my Mum, with love

First published in hardback in Great Britain by
HarperCollins Publishers Ltd in 1996
10 9 8 7 6 5 4 3 2 1
ISBN: 0 00 198128 5
First published in Picture Lions in 1996
Picture Lions is an imprint of the Children's Division,
part of HarperCollins Publishers Limited,
77-85 Fulham Palace Road, Hammersmith,
London W6 8JB
10 9 8
ISBN: 0 00 664519 4
Copyright © Joanna Harrison 1996
The author asserts the moral right to
be identified as the author of the work.
A CIP catalogue record for this title
is available from the British Library.
All rights reserved. No part of this publication
may be reproduced, stored in a retrieval system,
or transmitted in any form or by any means,
electronic, mechanical, photocopying, recording
or otherwise, without the prior permission of
HarperCollins Publishers Limited.
Printed and bound in Singapore.

We were having breakfast when the phone rang.
"Hello," said Mum. "Hi!... yes... yes... four o'clock...
lovely!... no... no problem... bye."

"**Arrrgh!**" she cried. "Your cousins are coming to tea!

The house is a mess and there's nothing to eat."

"Oh no!" said Sam.

"Children, make your hair and comb your beds, and do it properly!"
"Yes, Mum," we groaned. We knew what she meant, she just wasn't quite herself.

Mum spent most of the morning cleaning the house.
There was lots to do...

washing up the breakfast things... polishing...

hoovering up the cat hairs...

and scrubbing out the loo.

Sam and I forgot all about making our beds.
We made a jungle camp instead.

We had a great time but I don't think Mum
was very pleased.

Then we all had to go to the supermarket.

"Will you two STOP fighting!" shouted Mum.

When we got there, we wanted some crisps
but Mum just kept saying no.

She was getting really cross.

So we told her she was horrible.

After a while, we got so fed up we went off to do our own shopping. We were just beginning to enjoy ourselves when suddenly...

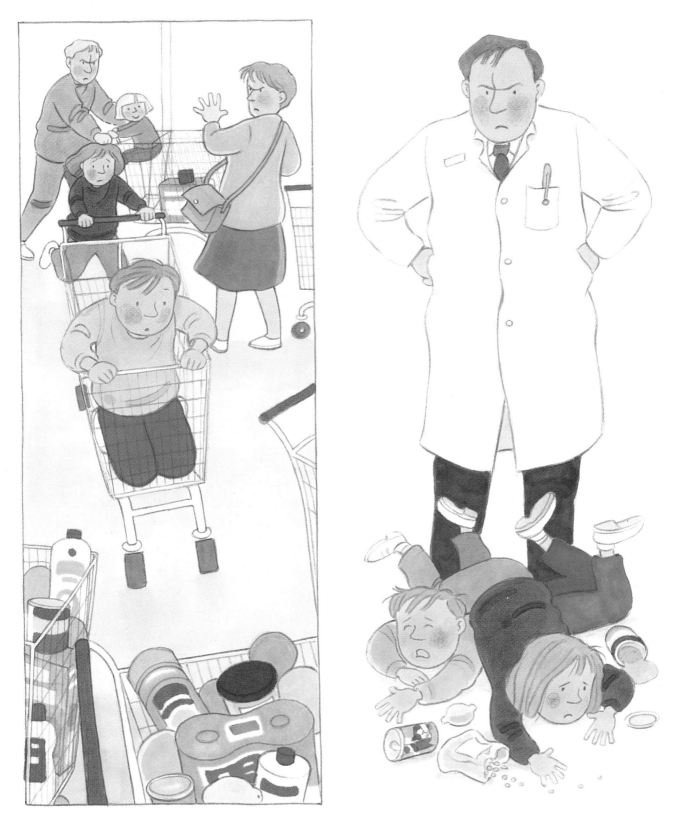

we crashed into some trolleys. I looked up to see
a man standing over us.
"And WHERE is your mother?" he asked angrily.

"HERE!" growled Mum.

Mum wouldn't let us have any sweets so I started to cry.
Sam told me to be quiet because everyone was looking at us...

so I cried even more, and Sam joined in.

When we got home, Mum unpacked the
shopping while we tried to make a cake.

But we made such a mess that Mum told
us to keep out of her way.

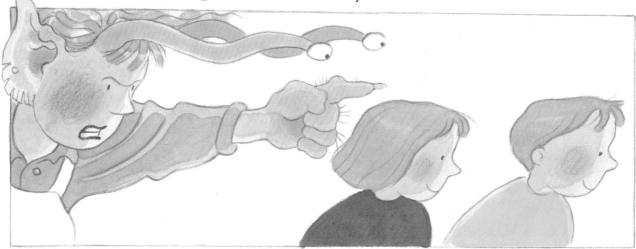

So Sam and I made an adventure playground on the
lawn. It was lots of fun going round on our bikes.
"It's lovely and muddy!" said Sam.

When it started to rain, we came inside.

Mum had laid tea out on the table. It looked
so delicious, we just had to help ourselves.

It was only after we'd eaten seven sandwiches, four iced buns, ten biscuits and most of the chocolate off the top of the cake, that we realised Mum might not be too pleased. So we ran upstairs to hide.

"What a mess!" said Sam, stuffing a
half-eaten sandwich into his pocket.

Then we heard footsteps... clomp... clomp... clomp...
coming up the stairs.

We dived under the bedclothes.

Sam looked at his watch. It was nearly four o'clock.

Suddenly the door burst open. I had never seen Mum looking THIS cross before! She tried to shout, but all

that came out was smoke and flames and a terrible roar.
"Oh no," whispered Sam. "She's gone completely BONKERS!"

But Mum just slumped into a chair.
"I used to be a nice person," she moaned. "But
all your mess and fighting, whinging and yelling,
has turned me... sob... into... sob... A MONSTER!"

Poor Mum! We didn't know what to say. So we
decided to tidy our room and make the beds.

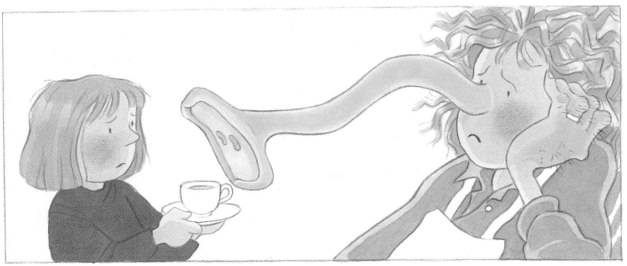

I gave Mum a cup of tea and we cleared away
our coats and boots, and hoovered the floor.

We put our bikes in the garage...

and made some more sandwiches.

We were just brushing our
hair when Mum came in.

"I'm sorry," she said. "I've been such a monster."
"Oh Mum," we both cried, "we're sorry too."

And we hugged each other tight.
Suddenly the door bell rang...

The cousins had arrived!

As Mum went downstairs to open the door,
we suddenly realised that she still had
monstrous hair!

Luckily we warned her just in time.

Well, we made it...

Aunt Jane seemed impressed.
"Darling!" she said. "Everything looks wonderful.
I do hope it wasn't too much trouble."
"Oh, it was nothing," murmured Mum.

At teatime our cousins were awful. They were such monsters they didn't even notice that their mum had grown...

a long... green... tail!